Dear Parent:
Your child's love of reading starts here!

Every child learns to read in a different way and at his or her own speed. Some go back and forth between reading levels and read favorite books again and again. Others read through each level in order. You can help your young reader improve and become more confident by encouraging his or her own interests and abilities. From books your child reads with you to the first books he or she reads alone, there are I Can Read Books for every stage of reading:

SHARED READING
Basic language, word repetition, and whimsical illustrations, ideal for sharing with your emergent reader

BEGINNING READING
Short sentences, familiar words, and simple concepts for children eager to read on their own

READING WITH HELP
Engaging stories, longer sentences, and language play for developing readers

READING ALONE
Complex plots, challenging vocabulary, and high-interest topics for the independent reader

ADVANCED READING
Short paragraphs, chapters, and exciting themes for the perfect bridge to chapter books

I Can Read Books have introduced children to the joy of reading since 1957. Featuring award-winning authors and illustrators and a fabulous cast of beloved characters, I Can Read Books set the standard for beginning readers.

A lifetime of discovery begins with the magical words **"I Can Read!"**

Visit www.icanread.com for information
on enriching your child's reading experience.

Pete the Cat's Groovy Bake Sale.
Text Copyright © 2018 by James Dean and Kimberly Dean. Art Copyright © 2018 by James Dean. Pete the Cat is a registered trademark of Pete the Cat, LLC. All rights reserved. Printed in the United States of America. No part of this book may be used or reproduced in any manner whatsoever without written permission except in the case of brief quotations embodied in critical articles and reviews. For information address HarperCollins Children's Books, a division of HarperCollins Publishers, 195 Broadway, New York, NY 10007.
www.icanread.com

Library of Congress Control Number: 2017959291
ISBN 978-0-06-267525-5 (trade bdg.) —ISBN 978-0-06-267524-8 (pbk.)

The artist used pen and ink, with watercolor and acrylic paint on 300lb hot press paper to create the illustrations for this book.

18 19 20 21 22   LSCC   10 9 8 7 6 5 4 3 2 1   ❖   First Edition

Pete the Cat is excited about
his school bake sale.

Pete wants to bake a treat.

What should Pete bake?

Pete loves sweets.

Pete loves cookies.
Pete loves pies.

Pete loves brownies, cakes,
marshmallow treats,
and ice-cream sundaes.

"I'll make cookies!"
Pete thinks.

Pete takes out eggs,
flour, sugar, and of course,
chocolate chips.

He puts everything in a bowl.

He stirs and stirs.

Pete makes a big mess!

He rolls the dough into balls,
and his mom helps put them
into the oven.

They wait for the cookies
to bake.
They smell so yummy.

Then things smell less yummy.
Some of the cookies
are burned!

Pete has to start over.

What else can he make?

He tries to make
ice-cream sundaes,
but they turn into
ice-cream soup.

He tries to make
pudding pie
but runs out of crust.

The kitchen is a big mess.
He has no treats
for the bake sale.

"You'll find something yummy
to bring to the bake sale,"
says Pete's mom.

He has some berries,
vanilla pudding,
and a few cookie pieces.

"I've got it!" Pete says.
"I'll use a little bit
of all of it!"

So he adds whipped cream and
berries to the pudding and stirs.

Then he adds some cookie
pieces to the mix.

Carefully, he scoops some
onto a tray.

Pete puts the tray in the fridge.

The next morning,
it is a tray of tasty, groovy
berry goodness!

His mom helps him
scoop his treats into little cups.
He brings them to school.

Pete puts his berry cups
on the bake sale table.

"What is that?" asks Callie.
"Groovy berry goodness!"
says Pete.

His friends give it a try.

His dessert is a hit!

Soon all the treats are gone.

But Pete saves one.

He gives it to his mom.

"Thanks for your help!"